You can be Anything!

This book is dedicated to children everywhere.
GC

Published in 2006 by Elora Media, LLC
Yelm, Washington

Text Copyright © Gary Craig 2004
Illustrations Copyright © Gary Craig 2006

The illustrations for this book were painted with watercolor and drawn in ink.
The text was set in Garamond.

For information contact:
Elora Media, LLC
PMB 112, 1201 Yelm Avenue
Yelm, Washington 98597
www.eloramedia.com

Library of Congress Cataloging-in-Publication Data available.

Summary:
The lyrical and charming verse in *You Can Be Anything!* encourages young readers to believe in themselves and their dreams.
With its heart-warming text and spirited illustrations, it's the perfect picture book to inspire children over and over again.

Printed and bound in the USA
ISBN 10-digit: 0-9786813-1-2
ISBN 13-digit: 978-0-9786813-1-9

You can be Anything!

Written & Illustrated by Gary Craig

AN ELORA MEDIA BOOK

eloraMEDIA
expanding minds

It's important to know

that whoever you are

all of life is a gift

and each child is a star.

And each star shines so bright

with a will that is free

that whatever you want

that is what you can be.

Whatever you dream in your heart

and your mind

if you hold your dream there then one day

you will find that your dream has come true

and the truth is, you see, that whatever you want

that is what you will be.

Don't listen to people who say that you can't

and shut your ears tight when they reason and rant.

For no one ever knows

who you are deep inside

so hold on to your dream.

Let your dream be your guide.

You will know on the day

that your dream becomes true

that the reason it came

was that you believed YOU.

In that moment of joy

when your heart starts to sing

then you'll know without doubt

YOU CAN BE ANYTHING!

Other Books by Gary Craig

Where Does the Sun Go?

I Can Be Anything Creative Activity Book

www.eloramedia.com